I Can Bearly Wait
A Child Learns Patience

"Be patient with everyone."
1 Thessalonians 5:14

Learning patience is a difficult achievement for adults—and even more so for children. *I Can Bearly Wait* helps young children to see the need for learning patience as a life skill through the experiences of Bear Lee.

D1616657

A BEAR HUGS BOOK ™

Love Bears All Things: A Child Learns to Love

Bear Up: A Child Learns to Handle Ups and Downs

Bearing Burdens: A Child Learns to Help

Bear Buddies: A Child Learns to Make Friends

Bearing Fruit: A Child Learns About the Fruit of the Spirit

I Can Bearly Wait: A Child Learns Patience

Titles in Preparation:

Bears Repeating: A Child Learns Thankfulness

You are Beary Special: A Child Learns Self-esteem

Bear Necessities: A Child Learns Obedience

Bear Facts: A Child Learns Truthfulness

Bearing Good News: A Child Learns to Be Positive

Sweeter Than Honey: A Child Learns the Golden Rule

Copyright 1987, Paul C. Brownlow
ISBN: 0-915720-63-9

All rights reserved. It is illegal to reproduce any part of this
book for any reason without the publisher's written consent.

Brownlow Publishing Company, Inc.
6309 Airport Freeway, Fort Worth, Texas 76117

I Can Bearly Wait
A Child Learns Patience

By

Pat Kirk & Alice Brown

Illustrated by

Diann Bartnick

BROWNLOW PUBLISHING COMPANY, INC.

The sun was just waking up. It was ready to tap the world on the shoulder as if to say, "Wake up, sleepy heads." But Bear Lee, the bear who could barely wait, was already awake.

Bear Lee threw back the covers of his rumpled bed and sprang out faster than a piece of crispy toast popping up from a sizzling toaster. Snoozy, his little brother, was still in bed dreaming about honey dripping from a honey jar onto his little pink tongue.

Yes, Snoozy was just as slow moving as the last drop of honey working its way down from the bottom to the top of an upside down jar. But, at least, he never got into much trouble.

Bear Lee just couldn't take the time to make up his
bed! He threw off his pajamas and tossed them into the

air faster than a honey bee doing a
dizzy dance for a parade of buzzing buddies.

The pajamas landed, much to his surprise, on the
ceiling fan right above his impatient little head. Round
and round his pajamas spun like carefree children
hanging onto a whizzing merry-go-round. "Oh, well,"
thought Bear Lee, "I won't need them until tonight. I'll
worry about that later."

Bear Lee ran down the steps to the kitchen. First, one step at a time; then, two; then, three. Kerplunk! Down rolled Bear Lee, the rest of the way, to the bottom! Good for him that his fur was thick and padded with plenty of bear underneath, fattened by licking many jars of rich, delicious, golden honey.

Mom was already in the kitchen cooking Bear
Lee's breakfast—honey pancakes oozing
with creamy melted butter
—his favorite!

"Bear Lee!" she scolded, gently.
"Your dad and I named you well. You
can barely wait for anything! You must learn
to be patient. You must think before you do things!"

Bear Lee could hear his mother talking, but he just couldn't take the time right then to really listen carefully to her wise words.

He gulped down his pancakes and slurped his milk, leaving traces of both on the table, and floor and, especially, on himself. He rustled out the door to play, leaving a honey trail all the way out onto the porch. "I'll clean up later," he thought.

Some hungry bees were in a thirsty flower bed, just outside the door. Buzz! Buzz! As soon as they saw the honey drenched cub, they swarmed after him, faster than the whizzing water sprinkler watering the lawn. Bear Lee saw them, too.

"Yipes!" he squealed, as he raced to the closest pond with the bees buzzing closely, too closely, behind him.

He jumped in with a splash, holding his scared little bear breath! He hid under the water until the confused bees flew away. Safe at last!

He was almost out of breath and wringing wet from head to paw. "No time to clean up," thought Bear Lee. "This water will just keep me cool all day. I might not even have to take a bath tonight."

But now Bear Lee was lonesome. He ran right to Buffy Bear's house. The thought of enjoying a game of tag with his friend on this beautiful sunshiny day made him run even faster.

One excited, soggy paw rang the doorbell. Bong. No one came. Bear Lee squirmed impatiently. So he rang again and again. Bong! Bong!

Still no one came. The third time he just kept his quivering paw stuck securely to the doorbell.

Bong!

Bong!

Bong!

Bong!

Bong!

Finally, someone shuffled to the door. It was
Mr. Gruff, Buffy's father. He opened the door slowly. He
looked down at Bear Lee who was feeling quite small.
Mr. Gruff frowned as he grabbed at a towel hugging his
soggy, furry waist.

"I guess I'm not the only wet bear around," thought
Bear Lee. Mr. Gruff growled, "Buffy is sick today. He
can't play. I hope you didn't wake him. We were up all
night giving him Bearitol."

"Oops, sorry," said Bear Lee.

Mr. Gruff slammed the door. Bear Lee left the porch so quickly that he knocked over several pot plants Mrs. Gruff had been taking care of all spring. "Uh oh," mumbled Bear Lee. "I really must learn to take my time and be more patient. I better clean up this mess."

But just at that very minute a beautiful yellow fluttering butterfly caught Bear Lee's eye. He completely forgot about the flower pots as he began to chase the lovely flittering creature who seemed to be teasing, "catch me if you can."

Bear Lee could not catch the butterfly, but his fuzzy ears caught a tinkling sound in the distance.

The music played louder and louder as it got closer and closer. Bear Lee knew that tune! It was the sweet song of the Lullabye Ice Cream Truck, bearing all kinds of delicious frozen sweet treats. Yum!

Bear Lee could barely wait! He ran all the way home —fur flying, tongue hanging out, taste buds clapping, straight to his very own house.

   Cars were parked all around it, in the driveway, and
on both sides of the street. Without stopping to think,
Bear Lee barged right through the front door as fast as
he could.

There was his mother, standing in the living room, holding a large plastic bottle and talking to a bunch of ladies who were listening carefully. Bear Lee interrupted her.

"Mom! Mom! Give me some bear bucks right now before the ice cream truck drives away," he sputtered, sticking an empty, wet paw right in her face.

"I can't get your money now, Bear Lee," mother said. "I'm showing these ladies how to store honey in these wonderful air tight jars that won't crack, break or chip." Bear Lee clapped his paws impatiently and began to whine and beg shamelessly. The lady bears pretended not to notice.

"I must send you to your room, Bear Lee," Mom commanded sternly, pointing her paw in that direction.

Reluctantly, Bear Lee shuffled, sobbing, to his room.
It just hadn't been his day. His unmade bed and flying
pajamas were there to greet him upon his arrival.

Snoozy's part of the room was as neat and clean as

a honeycomb. Snoozy was smacking on honey cakes Mother had baked for refreshments for the Fantastic Plastic Party. Several other munching cubs belonging to the party guests were sharing them with him. No, they didn't have an extra one for Bear Lee.

Things got even worse! That night, after supper, the phone rang. It was Mrs. Gruff. She insisted that Bear Lee come right over to clean up the mess that he had made on her front porch.

Mom and Dad thanked her for calling and sent Bear Lee right over. This time Bear Lee was not moving so quickly. He was really tired.

He apologized to Mr. and Mrs. Gruff and cleaned up their porch. He explained to them that he had not meant to be so much trouble; he was just in a hurry! He forgot to be patient.

When Bear Lee got home, he took his bath, swept his
pajamas off the ceiling fan with mother's broom and
went straight to bed. Mom and Dad came up to tuck
him in. "Tomorrow will be a better day," they said.

"Tomorrow I will think before I do anything," said Bear Lee. "I will start being patient."

"We know you will, son," they said, as they patted him on the head and turned off the light.

The moon was shining in the sun's place now, just as God planned. As Bear Lee lay looking at the soft twinkling stars, he noticed the moon did not seem to be in any hurry. He was so glad that Dad reminded him that God was patient.

From now on, Bear Lee decided, he would not be in a hurry, either. If God could wait, he could, too. He would be a patient bear, as God's word says to be. He would be Bear Lee, the patient, thinking bear.